A word is dead
When it is said,
  Some say.
I say it just
Begins to live
  That day.

SELECTED POEMS OF
EMILY Dickinson

A TOM DOHERTY ASSOCIATES BOOK
NEW YORK

This is a work of fiction. All the characters and events portrayed in this book are fictitious, and any resemblance to real people or events is purely coincidental.

SELECTED POEMS OF EMILY DICKINSON

Cover art by Mitchell Heinze

A Tor Book
Published by Tom Doherty Associates, Inc.
175 Fifth Avenue
New York, N.Y. 10010

Tor ® is a registered trademark of Tom Doherty Associates, Inc.

ISBN: 0-812-52338-5

First Tor edition: February 1993

Printed in the United States of America

0 9 8 7 6 5

Author's Biography

The story of Emily Elizabeth Dickinson is easy to tell. She was born in 1830 to a prominent family in Amherst, Massachusetts. Her father was a lawyer and legislator (elected to the Massachusetts State Senate in 1842 and to the House of Representatives in 1852). Her mother, Emily Norcross Dickinson, was a good housekeeper but, according to her first-born daughter, a passive woman who did "not care for thought." The poet's household included older brother Austin (born 1829) and younger sister Lavinia (1833) (as well as a beloved dog, Carlo, and Lavinia's brood of cats, which Emily despised). Austin married Emily's close friend Susan Gilbert in 1856, and the couple lived next door and maintained daily contact with the Dickinson household.

She attended Amherst Academy and spent a year at Mount Holyoke Female Seminary, but her education was gathered chiefly by reading books from her father's library. Her favorite reading included the Bible, Shakespeare, the poetry of John Keats and of Elizabeth Barrett Browning, as well as newspapers, journals and the popular novels of the day. A religious revival gripped much of Massachusetts in the 1840s and 1850s, but Dickinson maintained a stance of uncomfortable but uncompromising skepticism while many of her friends became believers and urged her to join the fold. She preferred to "keep the Sabbath" by "staying at home."

Aside from a few short trips in her twenties, Dickinson lived in the family house on Amherst's Main Street nearly her entire life. With her sister Lavinia (and a small group of servants, which even the moderately well-off could afford at that time), she ran the household. Both daughters of the house turned into the caretakers, keeping house for their father until his death in 1874, nursing their mother from the first failure in her health (1855) until her death in 1882. Between domestic tasks like baking bread and gardening, Emily was able to spend time at a small writing desk in her westward-facing bedroom on the second floor. In May of 1886 she was carried from her deathbed out of the house and across the fields for burial in the Dickinson plot not far away. It was not until after her death that even her sister learned just how much time she spent at her desk and what she did there.

Dickinson's story is also hard to tell. To outline her life is to list a good many things she did *not* do. She did not marry. Except for a brief trip to Boston to consult an eye specialist and brief trips to Philadelphia and Washington, D.C., she did not travel. She did not publish a book of poems, although a handful of poems appeared in print in her lifetime. The bare-bones facts of this quiet life make it sound like a career of denial, austerity, doing without. The legend that has grown from these facts—her habit of dressing in white, of secluding herself upstairs even when guests she liked came to call—makes her seem quirky, almost a freak. Yet the extraordinary poetry that emerged from this uneventful life—not in spite of it—attests to its richness, depth, and reflectiveness.

And it is hard to separate the legend of Emily Dickinson, recluse and eccentric, from the writings of Emily Dickinson, now recognized as one of the finest American poets who ever lived. First, let's not exaggerate the legend. Dickinson's house, often described as isolated, actually looked out onto a main street in a small but thriving college town. She numbered among her friends many prominent figures in the publishing world, such as Thomas Wentworth Higginson (who ushered her poems into print after her death), newspaperman Samuel Bowles, editor of the *Springfield Republi-*

can, and novelist and poet Helen Hunt Jackson. Her early letters reveal a precocious, witty teenager and young woman. As an adult she remained engaged with the world outside her doorstep through a large correspondence and wide reading.

But the most crucial part of the Dickinson legend takes place after her death. Her sister Lavinia discovered a locked box full of sheets of letter paper (some bound into little booklets), on which Dickinson had written a lifetime of short poems. Four years after her death, Higginson and Emily's Amherst neighbor Mabel Loomis Todd edited the first selection from her poems. New collections continued to appear throughout the 1890s, but in all these early editions, the poems were tidied up and made somewhat more conventional. It was not until 1955 that an edition of Dickinson's poetry was available, based closely on the poet's own manuscripts and placing poems roughly in the order in which they were written.

—Debra Fried,
Cornell University

Preface

Although she had been writing verse for some years, at about the age of thirty Emily Dickinson was ready to declare her vocation as a poet. In April 1862 she read in the newly-founded *Atlantic Monthly* an article by Thomas Wentworth Higginson called "Letter to a Young Contributor." The article offered aspiring writers a pep talk about the lofty challenges of writing, but chiefly gave down-to-earth practical advice (proofread carefully, use good paper, neatness counts). As though the article really were a letter addressed to her, Dickinson wrote a letter back to Higginson. It begins: "Are you too deeply occupied to say if my Verse is alive?" She enclosed four poems (one of them is in this book: "I'll tell you how the sun rose").

What are we to think of Dickinson's private response to what was patently a public "letter"? She called her poems her "Letter to the World." Although a published collection of Dickinson's poems did not appear in her lifetime, she sent poems to chosen correspondents, with friend Susan Gilbert Dickinson, who married her brother Austin in 1856, receiving the largest number of poems. The Austin Dickinsons lived next door, and for years Emily sent poems across the hedge to her sister-in-law, usually carried by one of the household servants. Often the poems were offhand, witty notes composed to accompany a small gift—a flower, bread. But others were drafts from Dickinson's growing sheaf of poems, and she solicited and valued Susan's opinion. Was the lifelong posting of poems in letters, poems as letters, a kind of private publication for Dickinson?

We cannot be sure, but reading Dickinson's poetry can sometimes feel like peeping in on a private correspondence. Her poetry is both simple and complicated, forthright and cloaked. Before beginning study of Dickinson's poetry, it helps to have a clear idea of the challenge—and the pleasure—ahead of you. What makes so many of these short poems so elusive?

First, Dickinson never finished them. She never gave a printer instructions about how she preferred them to be set into type. In this book, as in every published version of Dickinson's poetry, we are reading an editor's interpretation of a poet's private papers. The odd use of dashes you'll find in some of the poems probably reflects their unfinished surface (the same dashes appear in her letters and even in her recipes). But we will never be certain what, if anything, these characteristic penstrokes mean. Many of the poems are hard to distinguish from brilliant but perfunctory jottings, for much of what Lavinia Dickinson found locked away after her sister's death are unrevised drafts. The scattered look of "The Bobolink is gone"—the messiest poem in this book—is probably not an experimental verse form, but a working draft that dissolves into suggestive fragments. The tidier poems have been groomed by her first editors. Most of the manuscripts include the poet's second thoughts and lists of trial substitutions for individual words. To come up with a publishable version, an editor has had to make decisions about word choice that the writer herself did not make, and perhaps did not intend to make. For we cannot even be sure that our idea of a "finished" poem is the same as Dickinson's.

The poems are untitled. For convenience, we can refer to them by their first lines, but these are just handy tags for identification, not titles that contribute to our response to the poem. The editors of the 1890s compilations assigned their own titles to many of the poems.

The poems stretch the boundaries of language in their attempt to fathom mysteries or see things from a new angle. What kind of peculiar English is "A dew" and "the

Either" ("The spirit lasts—but in what mode")? Who but Dickinson would write of a "beryl apron" (in "It sounded as if the streets were running"), "winds" that are "prosy" ("I held a jewel in my fingers"), and winter becoming "An infinite Alas" ("The Dandelion's pallid tube")? Dickinson attaches peculiar adjectives to unlikely nouns: "sterile perquisite" ("To lose thee—sweeter than to gain"), "Eider—names" ("I went to Heaven"); sometimes these pairings create contradictions or paradoxes: "shrill felicity" ("No Brigadier throughout the Year").

Sometimes Dickinson seems to be inventing a new language, writing English "incorrectly" in order to capture her vision. Consider such odd expressions as "Our pace took sudden awe" ("Our journey had advanced") and "I became alone" ("The wind tapped like a tired man"), or comparing things by holding them "blue to blue" ("The brain is wider than the sky"). Even an ordinary little word like "of" can sound strange, as in "firm conviction of a mouse" ("The way I read a letter's this") or "Duties—of Gossamer" ("I went to Heaven"). She captures a spider in an intricate web of nouns: "Of immortality / His strategy / Was physiognomy" ("A spider sewed at night"). After reading a number of Dickinson's poems, though, these idiosyncracies come to seem essential rather than erroneous. Becoming familiar with Dickinson's writing is a bit like learning a new dialect, if not a new language.

The poems often contradict each other. They reflect Dickinson's life-long wavering between a desire to believe the fantastic promises of Christian immortality, and a hard-headed skepticism that reveled more in the thrill of a sustained doubt than in bland acceptance of comfortable doctrines. But on the whole she seems to have felt that the promised bliss of an afterlife was upstaged by the wonders of mortal life on earth. Her humble holy trinity can be found in her garden: "In the name of the Bee— / And of the Butterfly— / And of the Breeze—Amen!" ("The Gentian weaves her fringes"). A poem that begins with a confident assertion that "This world is not conclusion; / A sequel stands beyond," soon admits that this remains more a "riddle" than a belief. In another poem speculating about heaven she declares "I'm glad I don't believe it." Some poems begin with a tormenting question: ("The Spirit lasts—but in what mode,") and others try out how unquestioning acceptance would feel: ("Going to heaven! / I don't know when, / Pray do not ask me how").

But her challenge to popular beliefs goes beyond religion. Nothing looks the same after she has reshaped it in a poem. Her poems often redefine words and the world with a rebellious twist or a surprising angle: "Fame is a fickle food"; "Presentiment—is that long Shadow—on the Lawn"; "Sleep is supposed to be ... The shutting of the eye," but she will not rest content with what things are "supposed to be." She often defines by opposites, insisting that the only way you can know about something is to experience not having it: "To disappear enhances"; "To lose thee—sweeter than to gain." When someone dies, the survivors look at the world with new awareness and clarity, as though death were a spotlight that makes life itself leap into prominence:

> We noticed smallest things—
> Things overlooked before,
> By this great light upon our minds
> Italicized, as 't were.
>
>   ("The last night that she lived")

While some poems watch by a deathbed or visit the graveyard, other poems suggest that the closest we can arrive to a knowledge of death is by experiencing losses and departures in our lives ("My life closed twice before its close"). A number of poems tell about losing something, whether something precious ("I had a guinea golden; / I lost it in the sand"; "I held a jewel in my fingers / And went to sleep"), or something ordinary, a drop of dew ("A dew suffered itself"), even the drift of a thought ("A thought went up my mind today"). Or she will boldly imagine what the greatest privation might feel like with the casual announcement, "I lost a world the other day."

Dickinson suggests that the act of grieving, of asking questions about loss and death, may provide a kind of answer ("The distance that the dead have gone"). Certainty relies on a sustained doubt. Faith involves believing in what you cannot see, in what you must take on faith:

> Not seeing, still we know—
> Not knowing, guess—
> Not guessing, smile and hide
> And half caress.

For Dickinson, guessing is a way of caressing (as she implies by rhyming these words). The quirky guessing involved in writing poems was her preferred method of approaching these teasing mysteries.

Dickinson expresses her religious skepticism most forcefully in poems that adopt the voice of a child. Like the little girl Pearl in Hawthorne's *The Scarlet Letter*, Dickinson's child speaker can ask—in all innocence—bold and basic inquiries of the adult world, and thereby put in question adults' complacent pieties. A number of poems are spoken by the voice of a well-meaning innocent who takes adults absolutely at their word. The grown-ups say that we go to heaven when we die. So, the child reasons, heaven must be a place, maybe a place like Amherst, Massachusetts: "I went to Heaven—/'Twas a small Town"). Grown-ups say that the grave is just a temporary home for the dead:

Dickinson imagines a dead child speaking from the grave still clinging innocently to what she's been told:

> The grave my little cottage is,
> Where "keeping house" for thee
> I make my parlor orderly
> And lay the marble tea.

Dickinson often makes fun of conventional beliefs. She scoffs at narrow-minded prigs by imagining how they would disapprove of a flashy butterfly ("The butterfly obtains / But little sympathy"). She defies accepted views of what is appropriate for women, throwing off the names society would give her, for "I've stopped being theirs." It is clearly a female speaker (she speaks of "my apron" and "my bodice") who goes on an enigmatic journey in "I started early, took my dog," and survives an encounter with an oceanic force that is described as male. Many of the poems admire self-sufficiency, recognizing that if "Captivity is consciousness," then "So's liberty."

But Dickinson's defiance cannot simply be located in her more outspoken poems. Her challenge to accepted thinking is mounted simply in the surprising way she talks about everything from blue jays, sunrises, and storms, to heaven, the mind, and poetry itself.

—Debra Fried,
Cornell University

A dew sufficed itself
  And satisfied a leaf,
And felt, 'how vast a destiny!
  How trivial is life!'

The sun went out to work,
  The day went out to play,
But not again that dew was seen
  By physiognomy.

Whether by day abducted,
  Or emptied by the sun
Into the sea, in passing,
  Eternally unknown.

A door just opened on a street—
  I, lost, was passing by—
An instant's width of warmth disclosed,
  And wealth, and company.

The door as sudden shut, and I,
  I, lost, was passing by,—
Lost doubly, but by contrast most,
  Enlightening misery.

A face devoid of love or grace,
A hateful, hard, successful face,
  A face with which a stone
Would feel as thoroughly at ease
As were they old acquaintances,—
  First time together thrown.

A light exists in spring
  Not present on the year
At any other period.
  When March is scarcely here

A color stands abroad
  On solitary hills
That science cannot overtake,
  But human nature *feels*.

It waits upon the lawn;
  It shows the furthest tree
Upon the furthest slope we know;
  It almost speaks to me.

Then, as horizons step,
  Or noons report away,
Without the formula of sound,
  It passes, and we stay:

A quality of loss
  Affecting our content,
As trade had suddenly encroached
  Upon a sacrament.

A little road not made of man,
Enabled of the eye,
Accessible to thill of bee,
Or cart of butterfly.

If town it have, beyond itself,
'T is that I cannot say;
I only sigh,—no vehicle
Bears me along that way.

A long, long sleep, a famous sleep
  That makes no show for dawn
By stretch of limb or stir of lid,—
  An independent one.

Was ever idleness like this?
  Within a hut of stone
To bask the centuries away
  Not once look up for noon?

A murmur in the trees to note,
  Not loud enough for wind;
A star not far enough to seek,
  Nor near enough to find;

A long, long yellow on the lawn,
  A hubbub as of feet;
Not audible, as ours to us,
  But dapperer, more sweet;

A hurrying home of little men
  To houses unperceived,—
All this, and more, if I should tell,
  Would never be believed.

Of robins in the trundle bed
  How many I espy
Whose nightgowns could not hide the wings,
  Although I heard them try!

But then I promised ne'er to tell;
  How could I break my word?
So go your way and I'll go mine,—
  No fear you'll miss the road.

A poor torn heart, a tattered heart,
That sat it down to rest,
Nor noticed that the ebbing day

[*no stanza break*]

4

Flowed silver to the west,
Nor noticed night did soft descend
Nor constellation burn,
Intent upon the vision
Of latitudes unknown.

The angels, happening that way,
This dusty heart espied;
Tenderly took it up from toil
And carried it to God.
There,—sandals for the barefoot;
There,—gathered from the gales,
Do the blue havens by the hand
Lead the wandering sails.

A sickness of this world it most occasions
  When best men die;
A wishfulness their far condition
  To occupy.

A chief indifference, as foreign
  A world must be
Themselves forsake contented,
  For Deity.

A something in a summer's day,
As slow her flambeaux burn away,
Which solemnizes me.

A something in a summer's noon,—
An azure depth, a wordless tune,
Transcending ecstasy.

And still within a summer's night
A something so transporting bright,
I clap my hands to see;

Then veil my too inspecting face,
Lest such a subtle, shimmering grace
Flutter too far for me.

The wizard-fingers never rest,
The purple brook within the breast
Still chafes its narrow bed;

Still rears the East her amber flag,
Guides still the sun along the crag
His caravan of red,

Like flowers that heard the tale of dews,
But never deemed the dripping prize
Awaited their low brows;

Or bees, that thought the summer's name
Some rumor of delirium
No summer could for them;

Or Arctic creature, dimly stirred
By tropic hint,—some travelled bird
Imported to the wood;

Or wind's bright signal to the ear,
Making that homely and severe,
Contented, known, before

The heaven unexpected came,
To lives that thought their worshipping
A too presumptuous psalm.

A spider sewed at night
Without a light
Upon an arc of white.
If ruff it was of dame
Or shroud of gnome,
Himself, himself inform.
Of immortality
His strategy
Was physiognomy.

A thought went up my mind to-day
That I have had before,
But did not finish,—some way back,
I could not fix the year.

Nor where it went, nor why it came
The second time to me,
Nor definitely what it was,
Have I the art to say.

But somewhere in my soul, I know
I've met the thing before;
It just reminded me—'t was all—
And came my way no more.

A throe upon the features
A hurry in the breath,
An ecstasy of parting
Denominated "Death,"—

An anguish at the mention,
Which, when to patience grown,
I've known permission given
To rejoin its own.

A train went through a burial gate,
A bird broke forth and sang,
And trilled, and quivered, and shook his throat
Till all the churchyard rang;

And then adjusted his little notes,
And bowed and sang again.
Doubtless, he thought it meet of him
To say good-by to men.

A word is dead
When it is said,
  Some say.
I say it just
Begins to live
  That day.

Afraid? Of whom am I afraid?
Not death; for who is he?
The porter of my father's lodge
As much abasheth me.

Of life? 'T were odd I fear a thing
That comprehendeth me
In one or more existences
At Deity's decree.

Of resurrection? Is the east
Afraid to trust the morn
With her fastidious forehead?
As soon impeach my crown!

After a hundred years
Nobody knows the place,—
Agony, that enacted there,
Motionless as peace.

Weeds triumphant ranged,
Strangers strolled and spelled
At the lone orthography
Of the elder dead.

Winds of summer fields
Recollect the way,—
Instinct picking up the key
Dropped by memory.

An altered look about the hills;
A Tyrian light the village fills;
A wider sunrise in the dawn;
A deeper twilight on the lawn;
A print of a vermilion foot;
A purple finger on the slope;
A flippant fly upon the pane;
A spider at his trade again;
An added strut in chanticleer;
A flower expected everywhere;
An axe shrill singing in the woods;
Fern-odors on untravelled roads,—
All this, and more I cannot tell,
A furtive look you know as well,
And Nicodemus' mystery
Receives its annual reply.

As far from pity as complaint,
  As cool to speech as stone,
As numb to revelation
  · As if my trade were bone.

As far from time as history,
  As near yourself to-day
As children to the rainbow's scarf,
  Or sunset's yellow play

To eyelids in the sepulchre.
  How still the dancer lies,
While color's revelations break,
  And blaze the butterflies!

As if some little Arctic flower
Upon the polar hem—
Went wandering down the Latitudes
Until it puzzled came
To continents of summer—
To firmaments of sun—
To strange, bright crowds of flowers—
And birds, of foreign tongue!
I say, As if this little flower
To Eden, wandered in—
What then? Why nothing,
Only, your inference therefrom!

Before you thought of spring,
Except as a surmise,
You see, God bless his suddenness,
A fellow in the skies
Of independent hues,
A little weather-worn,
Inspiriting habiliments
Of indigo and brown.

With specimens of song,
As if for you to choose,
Discretion in the interval,
With gay delays he goes
To some superior tree
Without a single leaf,
And shouts for joy to nobody
But his seraphic self!

Dare you see a soul at the white heat?
  Then crouch within the door.
Red is the fire's common tint;
  But when the vivid ore

Has sated flame's conditions,
  Its quivering substance plays
Without a color but the light
  Of unanointed blaze.

Least village boasts its blacksmith,
  Whose anvil's even din
Stands symbol for the finer forge
  That soundless tugs within,

Refining these impatient ores
  With hammer and with blaze,
Until the designated light
  Repudiate the forge.

Death is a dialogue between
The spirit and the dust.
"Dissolve," says Death. The Spirit, "Sir,
I have another trust."

Death doubts it, argues from the ground.
The Spirit turns away,
Just laying off, for evidence,
An overcoat of clay.

Drowning is not so pitiful
  As the attempt to rise.
Three times, 't is said, a sinking man
  Comes up to face the skies,
And then declines forever
  To that abhorred abode
Where hope and he part company,—
  For he is grasped of God.
The Maker's cordial visage,
  However good to see,
Is shunned, we must admit it,
  Like an adversity.

Each life converges to some centre
Expressed or still;
Exists in every human nature
A goal,

Admitted scarcely to itself, it may be,
Too fair
For credibility's temerity
To dare.

Adored with caution, as a brittle heaven,
To reach
Were hopeless as the rainbow's raiment
To touch,

Yet persevered toward, surer for the distance;
How high
Unto the saints' slow diligence
The sky!

Ungained, it may be, by a life's low venture,
But then,
Eternity enables the endeavoring
Again.

Experiment to me
Is every one I meet,
If it contain a kernel?
The figure of a nut

Presents upon a tree,
Equally plausibly;
But meat within is requisite,
To squirrels and to me.

Fame is a fickle food
Upon a shifting plate
Whose table once a
Guest but not
The second time is set.

Whose crumbs the crows inspect
And with ironic caw
Flap past it to the
Farmer's Corn
Men eat of it and die.

Fate slew him, but he did not drop;
  She felled—he did not fall—
Impaled him on her fiercest stakes—
  He neutralized them all.

She stung him, sapped his firm advance,
  But, when her worst was done,
And he, unmoved, regarded her,
  Acknowledged him a man.

Frequently the woods are pink,
Frequently are brown;
Frequently the hills undress
Behind my native town.

Oft a head is crested
I was wont to see,
And as oft a cranny
Where it used to be.

And the earth, they tell me,
On its axis turned,—
Wonderful rotation
By but twelve performed!

Given in marriage unto thee,
 Oh, thou celestial host!
Bride of the Father and the Son,
 Bride of the Holy Ghost!

Other betrothal shall dissolve,
 Wedlock of will decay;
Only the keeper of this seal
 Conquers mortality.

Going to heaven!
I don't know when,
Pray do not ask me how,—
Indeed, I'm too astonished
To think of answering you!
Going to heaven!—
How dim it sounds!
And yet it will be done
As sure as flocks go home at night
Unto the shepherd's arm!

Perhaps you're going too!
Who knows?
If you should get there first,
Save just a little place for me
Close to the two I lost!
The smallest "robe" will fit me,
And just a bit of "crown;"
For you know we do not mind our dress
When we are going home.

I'm glad I don't believe it,
For it would stop my breath,
And I'd like to look a little more
At such a curious earth!
I am glad they did believe it
Whom I have never found
Since the mighty autumn afternoon
I left them in the ground.

Good night! which put the candle out?
A jealous zephyr, not a doubt.
  Ah! friend, you little knew
How long at that celestial wick
The angels labored diligent;
  Extinguished, now, for you!

It might have been the lighthouse spark
Some sailor, rowing in the dark,
  Had importuned to see!
It might have been the waning lamp
That lit the drummer from the camp
  To purer reveille!

Great streets of silence led away
To neighborhoods of pause;
Here was no notice, no dissent,
No universe, no laws.

By clocks 't was morning, and for night
The bells at distance called;
But epoch had no basis here,
For period exhaled.

Have you got a brook in your little heart,
Where bashful flowers blow,
And blushing birds go down to drink,
And shadows tremble so?

And nobody knows, so still it flows,
That any brook is there;
And yet your little draught of life
Is daily drunken there.

Then look out for the little brook in March,
When the rivers overflow,
And the snows come hurrying from the hills,
And the bridges often go.

And later, in August it may be,
When the meadows parching lie,
Beware, lest this little brook of life
Some burning noon go dry!

He ate and drank the precious Words—
His Spirit grew robust—
He knew no more that he was poor,
Nor that his frame was Dust—

He danced along the dingy Days
And this Bequest of Wings
Was but a Book—What Liberty
A loosened spirit brings—

He touched me, so I live to know
That such a day, permitted so,
  I groped upon his breast.
It was a boundless place to me,
And silenced, as the awful sea
  Puts minor streams to rest.

And now, I'm different from before,
As if I breathed superior air,
  Or brushed a royal gown;
My feet, too, that had wandered so,
My gypsy face transfigured now
  To tenderer renown.

Hope is a subtle glutton;
  He feeds upon the fair;
And yet, inspected closely,
  What abstinence is there!

His is the halcyon table
  That never seats but one,
And whatsoever is consumed
  The same amounts remain.

How dare the robins sing,
  When men and women hear
Who since they went to their account
  Have settled with the year!—
Paid all that life had earned
  In one consummate bill,
And now, what life or death can do
  Is immaterial.
Insulting is the sun
  To him whose mortal light,
Beguiled of immortality,
  Bequeaths him to the night.
In deference to him
  Extinct be every hum,
Whose garden wrestles with the dew,
  At daybreak overcome!

How happy is the little stone
That rambles in the road alone,
And doesn't care about careers,
And exigencies never fears;
Whose coat of elemental brown
A passing universe put on;
And independent as the sun,
Associates or glows alone,
Fulfilling absolute decree
In casual simplicity.

I cannot live with you,
It would be life,
And life is over there
Behind the shelf

The sexton keeps the key to,
Putting up
Our life, his porcelain,
Like a cup

Discarded of the housewife,
Quaint or broken;
A newer Sèvres pleases,
Old ones crack.

I could not die with you,
For one must wait
To shut the other's gaze down,—
You could not.

And I, could I stand by
And see you freeze,
Without my right of frost,
Death's privilege?

Nor could I rise with you,
Because your face
Would put out Jesus',
That new grace

Glow plain and foreign
On my homesick eye,
Except that you, than he
Shone closer by.

They'd judge us—how?
For you served Heaven, you know,
Or sought to;
I could not,

Because you saturated sight,
And I had no more eyes
For sordid excellence
As Paradise.

And were you lost, I would be,
Though my name
Rang loudest
On the heavenly fame.

And were you saved,
And I condemned to be
Where you were not,
That self were hell to me.

So we must keep apart,
You there, I here,
With just the door ajar
That oceans are,
And prayer,
And that pale sustenance,
Despair!

I did not reach Thee
But my feet slip nearer every day
Three Rivers and a Hill to cross
One Desert and a Sea
I shall not count the journey one
When I am telling thee

Two deserts but the Year is cold
So that will help the sand
One desert crossed—
The second one
Will feel as cool as land
Sahara is too little price
To pay for thy Right hand

The Sea comes last—Step merry feet
So short we have to go
To play together we are prone
But we must labor now
The last shall be the lightest load
That we have had to draw

The Sun goes crooked—
That is Night
Before he makes the bend
We must have passed the Middle Sea
Almost we wish the End
Were further off
Too great it seems
So near the Whole to stand

We step like Plush
We stand like snow
The waters murmur new
Three rivers and the Hill are passed
Two deserts and the sea!
Now Death usurps my Premium
And gets the look at Thee—

I felt a clearing in my mind
  As if my brain had split;
I tried to match it, seam by seam,
  But could not make them fit.

The thought behind I strove to join
  Unto the thought before,
But sequence ravelled out of reach
  Like balls upon a floor.

I gave myself to him,
And took himself for pay.
The solemn contract of a life
Was ratified this way.

The wealth might disappoint,
Myself a poorer prove
Than this great purchaser suspect:
The daily own of Love

Depreciates the vision;
But, till the merchant buy,
Still fable, in the isles of spice,
The subtle cargoes lie.

At least, 't is mutual risk,—
Some found it mutual gain;
Sweet debt of Life,—each night to owe,
Insolvent, every noon.

I had a guinea golden;
  I lost it in the sand,
And though the sum was simple,
  And pounds were in the land,
Still had it such a value
  Unto my frugal eye,
That when I could not find it
  I sat me down to sigh.

I had a crimson robin
  Who sang full many a day,
But when the woods were painted
  He, too, did fly away.
Time brought me other robins,—
  Their ballads were the same,—
Still for my missing troubadour
  I kept the 'house at hame.'

I had a star in heaven;
  One Pleiad was its name,
And when I was not heeding
  It wandered from the same.
And though the skies are crowded,
  And all the night ashine,
I do not care about it,
  Since none of them are mine.

My story has a moral:
  I have a missing friend,—
Pleiad its name, and robin,

[*no stanza break*]

26

And guinea in the sand,—
And when this mournful ditty,
  Accompanied with tear,
Shall meet the eye of traitor
  In country far from here,
Grant that repentance solemn
  May seize upon his mind,
And he no consolation
  Beneath the sun may find.

I had no cause to be awake,
My best was gone to sleep,
And morn a new politeness took,
And failed to wake them up,

But called the others clear,
And passed their curtains by.
Sweet morning, when I over-sleep,
Knock, recollect, for me!

I looked at sunrise once,
And then I looked at them,
And wishfulness in me arose
For circumstance the same.

'T was such an ample peace,
It could not hold a sigh,—
'T was Sabbath with the bells divorced,
'T was sunset all the day.

So choosing but a gown
And taking but a prayer,
The only raiment I should need,
I struggled, and was there.

I had no time to hate, because
The grave would hinder me,
And life was not so ample I
Could finish enmity.

Nor had I time to love; but since
Some industry must be,
The little toil of love, I thought,
Was large enough for me.

I held a jewel in my fingers
And went to sleep.
The day was warm, and winds were prosy;
I said: "'T will keep."

I woke and chid my honest fingers,—
The gem was gone;
And now an amethyst remembrance
Is all I own.

I like a look of Agony,
Because I know it's true—
Men do not sham Convulsion,
Nor simulate, a Throe—

The Eyes glaze once—and that is Death—
Impossible to feign
The Beads upon the Forehead
By homely Anguish strung.

I like to see it lap the miles,
And lick the valleys up,
And stop to feed itself at tanks;
And then, prodigious, step

Around a pile of mountains,
And, supercilious, peer
In shanties by the sides of roads;
And then a quarry pare

To fit its sides, and crawl between,
Complaining all the while
In horrid, hooting stanza;
Then chase itself down hill

And neigh like Boanerges;
Then, punctual as a star,
Stop—docile and omnipotent—
And its own stable door.

I lost a world the other day.
Has anybody found?
You'll know it by the row of stars
Around its forehead bound.

A rich man might not notice it;
Yet to my frugal eye
Of more esteem than ducats.
Oh, find it, sir, for me!

I meant to find her when I came;
   Death had the same design;
But the success was his, it seems,
   And the discomfit mine.

I meant to tell her how I longed
   For just this single time;
But Death had told her so the first,
   And she had hearkened him.

To wander now is my abode;
   To rest,—to rest would be
A privilege of hurricane
   To memory and me.

I read my sentence steadily,
Reviewed it with my eyes,
To see that I made no mistake
In its extremest clause,—

The date, and manner of the shame;
And then the pious form
That "God have mercy" on the soul
The jury voted him.

I made my soul familiar
With her extremity,
That at the last it should not be
A novel agony,

But she and Death, acquainted,
Meet tranquilly as friends,
Salute and pass without a hint—
And there the matter ends.

I started early, took my dog,
And visited the sea;
The mermaids in the basement
Came out to look at me,

And frigates in the upper floor
Extended hempen hands,
Presuming me to be a mouse
Aground, upon the sands.

But no man moved me till the tide
Went past my simple shoe,
And past my apron and my belt,
And past my bodice too,

And made as he would eat me up
As wholly as a dew
Upon a dandelion's sleeve—
And then I started too.

And he—he followed close behind;
I felt his silver heel
Upon my ankle,—then my shoes
Would overflow with pearl.

Until we met the solid town,
No man he seemed to know;
And bowing with a mighty look
At me, the sea withdrew.

I stepped from plank to plank
  So slow and cautiously;
The stars about my head I felt,
  About my feet the sea.

I knew not but the next
  Would be my final inch,—
This gave me that precarious gait
  Some call experience.

I think the hemlock likes to stand
Upon a marge of snow;
It suits his own austerity,
And satisfies an awe

That men must slake in wilderness,
Or in the desert cloy,—
An instinct for the hoar, the bald,
Lapland's necessity.

The hemlock's nature thrives on cold;
The gnash of northern winds
Is sweetest nutriment to him,
His best Norwegian wines.

To satin races he is nought;
But children on the Don
Beneath his tabernacles play,
And Dnieper wrestlers run.

I took my power in my hand
And went against the world;
'T was not so much as David had,
But I was twice as bold.

I aimed my pebble, but myself
Was all the one that fell.
Was it Goliath was too large,
Or only I too small?

I went to Heaven—
'Twas a small Town—
Lit—with a Ruby—
Lathed—with Down—

Stiller—than the fields
At the full Dew—
Beautiful—as Pictures—
No Man drew.
People—like the Moth—
Of Mechlin—frames—
Duties—of Gossamer—
And Eider—names—

[*no stanza break*]

Almost—contented—
I—could be—
'Mong such unique
Society—

I years had been from home,
And now, before the door,
I dared not open, lest a face
I never saw before

Stare vacant into mine
And ask my business there.
My business,—just a life I left,
Was such still dwelling there?

I fumbled at my nerve,
I scanned the windows near;
The silence like an ocean rolled,
And broke against my ear.

I laughed a wooden laugh
That I could fear a door,
Who danger and the dead had faced,
But never quaked before.

I fitted to the latch
My hand, with trembling care,
Lest back the awful door should spring,
And leave me standing there.

I moved my fingers off
As cautiously as glass,
And held my ears, and like a thief
Fled gasping from the house.

If I may have it when it's dead
   I will contented be;
If just as soon as breath is out
   It shall belong to me,

Until they lock it in the grave,
   'T is bliss I cannot weigh,
For though they lock thee in the grave,
   Myself can hold the key.

Think of it, lover! I and thee
   Permitted face to face to be;
After a life, a death we'll say,—
   For death was that, and this is thee.

If recollecting were forgetting,
   Then I remember not;
And if forgetting, recollecting,
   How near I had forgot!
And if to miss were merry,
   And if to mourn were gay,
How very blithe the fingers
   That gathered these to-day!

I'll tell you how the sun rose,—
A ribbon at a time.
The steeples swam in amethyst,
The news like squirrels ran.

The hills untied their bonnets,
The bobolinks begun.
Then I said softly to myself,
"That must have been the sun!"

. . . . . .

But how he set, I know not.
There seemed a purple stile
Which little yellow boys and girls
Were climbing all the while

Till when they reached the other side,
A dominie in gray
Put gently up the evening bars,
And led the flock away.

I'm ceded, I've stopped being theirs;
The name they dropped upon my face
With water, in the country church,
Is finished using now,
And they can put it with my dolls,
My childhood, and the string of spools
I've finished threading too.

Baptized before without the choice,
But this time consciously, of grace
Unto supremest name,
Called to my full, the crescent dropped,
Existence's whole arc filled up
With one small diadem.

My second rank, too small the first,
Crowned, crowing on my father's breast,
A half unconscious queen;
But this time, adequate, erect,
With will to choose or to reject,
And I choose—just a throne.

I'm nobody! Who are you?
Are you nobody, too?
Then there's a pair of us—don't tell!
They'd banish us, you know.

How dreary to be somebody!
How public, like a frog
To tell your name the livelong day
To an admiring bog!

Is bliss, then, such abyss
I must not put my foot amiss
For fear I spoil my shoe?

I'd rather suit my foot
Than save my boot,
For yet to buy another pair
Is possible
At any fair.

But bliss is sold just once;
The patent lost
None buy it any more.

It dropped so low—in my Regard—
I heard it hit the Ground—
And go to pieces on the Stones
At bottom of my Mind—

Yet blamed the Fate that fractured—*less*
Than I reviled Myself,
For entertaining Plated Wares
Upon my Silver Shelf—

It sounded as if the streets were running,
And then the streets stood still.
Eclipse was all we could see at the window,
And awe was all we could feel.

By and by the boldest stole out of his covert,
To see if time was there.
Nature was in her beryl apron,
Mixing fresher air.

It tossed and tossed,—
A little brig I knew,—
O'ertook by blast;
It spun and spun,
And groped delirious, for morn.

It slipped and slipped,
As one that drunken stepped;
Its white foot tripped,
Then dropped from sight.

Ah, brig, good-night
To crew and you;
The ocean's heart too smooth, too blue,
To break for you.

I've got an arrow here.
Loving the hand that sent it
I the dart revere.

Fell, they will say, in "skirmish"!
Vanquished, my soul will know
By but a simple arrow
Sped by an archer's bow.

I've seen a dying eye
Run round and round a room
In search of something, as it seemed,
Then cloudier become;
And then, obscure with fog,
And then be soldered down,
Without disclosing what it be,
'T were blessed to have seen.

Me! Come! My dazzled face
In such a shining place!

Me! Hear! My foreign ear
The sounds of welcome near!

The saints shall meet
Our bashful feet.

My holiday shall be
That they remember me;

My paradise, the fame
That they pronounce my name.

Mine by the right of the white election!
Mine by the royal seal!
Mine by the sign in the scarlet prison
Bars cannot conceal!

Mine, here in vision and in veto!
Mine, by the grave's repeal
Titled, confirmed,—delirious charter!
Mine, while the ages steal!

My cocoon tightens, colors tease,
I'm feeling for the air;
A dim capacity for wings
Degrades the dress I wear.

A power of butterfly must be
The aptitude to fly,
Meadows of majesty concedes
And easy sweeps of sky.

So I must baffle at the hint
And cipher at the sign,
And make much blunder, if at last
I take the clew divine.

My country need not change her gown,
Her triple suit as sweet
As when 't was cut at Lexington,
And first pronounced "a fit."

Great Britain disapproves "the stars;"
Disparagement discreet,—
There's something in their attitude
That taunts her bayonet.

My life closed twice before its close;
It yet remains to see
If Immortality unveil
A third event to me,

So huge, so hopeless to conceive
As these that twice befel.
Parting is all we know of heaven,
And all we need of hell.

My worthiness is all my doubt,
  His merit all my fear,
Contrasting which, my qualities
  Do lowlier appear;

Lest I should insufficient prove
  For his beloved need,
The chiefest apprehension
  Within my loving creed.

So I, the undivine abode
  Of his elect content,
Conform my soul as 't were a church
  Unto her sacrament.

Nature rarer uses yellow
  Than another hue;
Saves she all of that for sunsets,—
  Prodigal of blue,

Spending scarlet like a woman,
  Yellow she affords
Only scantly and selectly,
  Like a lover's words.

No Brigadier throughout the Year
So civic as the Jay—
A Neighbor and a Warrior too
With shrill felicity
Pursuing Winds that censure us
A February Day,
The Brother of the Universe
Was never blown away—

[no stanza break]

The Snow and he are intimate—
I've often seen them play
When Heaven looked upon us all
With such severity
I felt apology were due
To an insulted sky
Whose pompous frown was Nutriment
To their Temerity—
The Pillow of this daring Head
Is pungent Evergreens—
His Larder—terse and Militant—
Unknown—refreshing things—
His Character—a Tonic—
His Future—a Dispute—
Unfair an Immortality
That leaves this Neighbor out—

No rack can torture me,
My soul's at liberty.
Behind this mortal bone
There knits a bolder one

You cannot prick with saw,
Nor rend with scymitar.
Two bodies therefore be;
Bind one, and one will flee.

The eagle of his nest
No easier divest
And gain the sky,
Than mayest thou,

Except thyself may be
Thine enemy;
Captivity is consciousness,
So's liberty.

Not seeing, still we know—
Not knowing, guess—
Not guessing, smile and hide
And half caress—

And quake—and turn away,
Seraphic fear—
Is Eden's innuendo
"If you dare"?

One blessing had I, than the rest
    So larger to my eyes
That I stopped gauging, satisfied,
    For this enchanted size.

It was the limit of my dream,
    The focus of my prayer,—
A perfect, paralyzing bliss
    Contented as despair.

I knew no more of want or cold,
    Phantasms both become,
For this new value in the soul,
    Supremest earthly sum.

The heaven below the heaven above
  Obscured with ruddier hue.
Life's latitude leant over-full;
  The judgment perished, too.

Why joys so scantily disburse,
  Why Paradise defer,
Why floods are served to us in bowls,—
  I speculate no more.

One of the ones that Midas touched,
Who failed to touch us all,
Was that confiding prodigal,
The blissful oriole.

So drunk, he disavows it
With badinage divine;
So dazzling, we mistake him
For an alighting mine.

A pleader, a dissembler,
An epicure, a thief,—
Betimes an oratorio,
An ecstasy in chief;

The Jesuit of orchards,
He cheats as he enchants
Of an entire attar
For his decamping wants.

The splendor of a Burmah,
The meteor of birds,
Departing like a pageant
Of ballads and of bards.

I never thought that Jason sought
For any golden fleece;
But then I am a rural man,
With thoughts that make for peace.

But if there were a Jason,
Tradition suffer me
Behold his lost emolument
Upon the apple tree.

Our journey had advanced;
Our feet were almost come
To that odd fork in Being's road,
Eternity by term.

Our pace took sudden awe,
Our feet reluctant led.
Before were cities, but between,
The forest of the dead.

Retreat was out of hope,—
Behind, a sealed route,
Eternity's white flag before,
And God at every gate.

Presentiment—is that long Shadow—
  on the Lawn—
Indicative that Suns go down—

The Notice to the startled Grass
That Darkness—is about to pass—

Remembrance has a rear and front,—
  ' T is something like a house;
It has a garret also
  For refuse and the mouse,

Besides, the deepest cellar
  That ever mason hewed;
Look to it, by its fathoms
  Ourselves be not pursued.

Sleep is supposed to be
By souls of sanity
The shutting of the eye.

Sleep is the station grand
Down wh', on either hand
The hosts of witness stand!

Morn is supposed to be
By people of degree
The breaking of the Day.

Morning has not occurred!

That shall Aurora be—
East of Eternity—
One with the banner gay—
One in the red array—
That is the break of Day!

Softened by Time's consummate plush,
 How sleek the woe appears
That threatened childhood's citadel
 And undermined the years!

Bisected now by bleaker griefs,
 We envy the despair
That devastated childhood's realm,
 So easy to repair.

Some rainbow coming from the fair!
Some vision of the world Cashmere
I confidently see!
Or else a peacock's purple train,
Feather by feather, on the plain
Fritters itself away!

The dreamy butterflies bestir,
Lethargic pools resume the whir
Of last year's sundered tune.
From some old fortress on the sun
Baronial bees march, one by one,
In murmuring platoon!

The robins stand as thick to-day
As flakes of snow stood yesterday,
On fence and roof and twig.

[no stanza break]

The orchis binds her feather on
For her old lover, Don the Sun,
Revisiting the bog!

Without commander, countless, still,
The regiment of wood and hill
In bright detachment stand.
Behold! Whose multitudes are these?
The children of whose turbaned seas,
Or what Circassian land?

Superiority to fate
   Is difficult to learn.
' T is not conferred by any,
   But possible to earn

A pittance at a time,
   Until, to her surprise,
The soul with strict economy
   Subsists till Paradise.

The Bobolink is gone—   the Rowdy of the
   Meadow—
And no one swaggers now but me—
The Presbyterian Birds can now resume the
   Meeting
He gaily interrupted that overflowing Day
   boldly

[*no stanza break*]

When opening the Sabbath in their afflictive
    Way
He bowed to Heaven instead of Earth
            to every Heaven above
            to all the saints he knew
                every God he knew
And shouted Let us pray—
and bubbled let us pray—

He recognized his maker—overturned the
    Decalogue

He swung upon the Decalogue
And shouted Let us pray—

When supplicating mercy
In a portentous way—   portentous way

Gay from an unannointed Twig   Sweet
    from a surr
He gurgled—   Let us pray—
    bubbled

The brain is wider than the sky,
  For, put them side by side,
The one the other will include
  With ease, and you beside.

The brain is deeper than the sea,
  For, hold them, blue to blue,
The one the other will absorb,
  As sponges, buckets do.

The brain is just the weight of God,
  For, lift them, pound for pound,
And they will differ, if they do,
  As syllable from sound.

The butterfly obtains
But little sympathy
Though favorably mentioned
In Entomology—

Because he travels freely
And wea[r]s a proper coat
The circumspect are certain
That he is dissolute

Had he the homely scutcheon
Of modest Industry
T'were fitter certifying
For Immortality—

The cricket sang,
And set the sun,
And workmen finished, one by one,
  Their seam the day upon.

The low grass loaded with the dew,
The twilight stood as strangers do
With hat in hand, polite and new,
  To stay as if, or go.

A vastness, as a neighbor, came,—
A wisdom without face or name,
A peace, as hemispheres at home,—
  And so the night became.

The Dandelion's pallid tube
Astonishes the Grass,
And Winter instantly becomes
An infinite Alas—
The tube uplifts a signal Bud
And then a shouting Flower,—
The Proclamation of the Suns
That sepulture is o'er.

The distance that the dead have gone
Does not at first appear;
Their coming back seems possible
For many an ardent year.

And then, that we have followed them,
We more than half suspect,
So intimate have we become
With their dear retrospect.

The Gentian weaves her fringes—
The Maple's loom is red—
My departing blossoms
       Obviate parade.

A brief, but patient illness—
An hour to prepare,
And one below, this morning
Is where the angels are—
It was a short procession,
The Bobolink was there—
An aged Bee addressed us—
And then we knelt in prayer—
We trust that she was willing—
We ask that we may be.
Summer—Sister—Seraph!
Let us go with thee!

In the name of the Bee—
And of the Butterfly—
And of the Breeze—Amen!

The grave my little cottage is,
Where "Keeping house" for thee
I make my parlor orderly
And lay the marble tea.

For two divided, briefly,
A cycle, it may be,
Till everlasting life unite
In strong society.

The heart asks pleasure first,
And then, excuse from pain;
And then, those little anodynes
That deaden suffering;

And then, to go to sleep;
And then, if it should be
The will of its Inquisitor,
The liberty to die.

The last night that she lived,
It was a common night,
Except the dying; this to us
Made nature different.

We noticed smallest things,—
Things overlooked before,
By this great light upon our minds
Italicized, as 't were.

That others could exist
While she must finish quite,
A jealousy for her arose
So nearly infinite.

We waited while she passed;
It was a narrow time,
Too jostled were our souls to speak,
At length the notice came.

She mentioned, and forgot;
Then lightly as a reed
Bent to the water, shivered scarce,
Consented, and was dead.

And we, we placed the hair,
And drew the head erect;
And then an awful leisure was,
Our faith to regulate.

The longest day that God appoints
Will finish with the sun.
Anguish can travel to its stake,
And then it must return.

The reticent volcano keeps
His never slumbering plan;
Confided are his projects pink
To no precarious man.

If nature will not tell the tale
Jehovah told to her
Can human nature not survive
Without a listener?

Admonished by her buckled lips
Let every babbler be
The only secret people keep
Is Immortality.

The saddest noise, the sweetest noise,
  The maddest noise that grows,—
The birds, they make it in the spring,
  At night's delicious close.

Between the March and April line—
  That magical frontier
Beyond which summer hesitates,
  Almost too heavenly near.

It makes us think of all the dead
  That sauntered with us here,
By separation's sorcery
  Made cruelly more dear.

It makes us think of what we had,
  And what we now deplore.
We almost wish those siren throats
  Would go and sing no more.

An ear can break a human heart
  As quickly as a spear,
We wish the ear had not a heart
  So dangerously near.

The soul unto itself
Is an imperial friend,—
Or the most agonizing spy
An enemy could send.

Secure against its own,
No treason it can fear;
Itself its sovereign, of itself
The soul should stand in awe.

The Spirit lasts—but in what mode—
Below, the Body speaks,
But as the Spirit furnishes—
Apart, it never talks—
The Music in the Violin
Does not emerge alone
But Arm in Arm with Touch, yet Touch
Alone—is not a Tune—
The Spirit lurks within the Flesh
Like Tides within the Sea
That make the Water live, estranged
What would the Either be?
Does that know—now—or does it cease—
That which to this is done,
Resuming at a mutual date
With every future one?

[*no stanza break*]

Instinct pursues the Adamant,
Exacting this Reply—
Adversity if it may be, or
Wild Prosperity,
The Rumor's Gate was shut so tight
Before my Mind was sown,
Not even a Prognostic's Push
Could make a Dent thereon—

The Sun kept setting—setting—still
No Hue of Afternoon—
Upon the Village I perceived—
From House to House 'twas Noon—

The Dusk kept dropping—dropping—still
No Dew upon the Grass—
But only on my Forehead stopped—
And wandered in my Face—

My Feet kept drowsing—drowsing—still
My fingers were awake—
Yet why so little sound—Myself
Unto my Seeming—make?

How well I knew the Light before—
I could not see it now—
'Tis Dying—I am doing—but
I'm not afraid to know—

The way I read a letter's this:
'T is first I lock the door,
And push it with my fingers next,
For transport it be sure.

And then I go the furthest off
To counteract a knock;
Then draw my little letter forth
And softly pick its lock.

Then, glancing narrow at the wall,
And narrow at the floor,
For firm conviction of a mouse
Not exorcised before,

Peruse how infinite I am
To—no one that you know!
And sigh for lack of heaven,—but not
The heaven the creeds bestow.

The wind tapped like a tired man,
And like a host, "Come in,"
I boldly answered; entered then
My residence within

A rapid, footless guest,
To offer whom a chair
Were as impossible as hand
A sofa to the air.

No bone had he to bind him,
His speech was like the push
Of numerous humming-birds at once
From a superior bush.

His countenance a billow,
His fingers, if he pass,
Let go a music, as of tunes
Blown tremulous in glass.

He visited, still flitting;
Then, like a timid man,
Again he tapped—'t was flurriedly—
And I became alone.

Their height in heaven comforts not,
Their glory nought to me;
'T was best imperfect, as it was;
I'm finite, I can't see.

The house of supposition,
The glimmering frontier
That skirts the acres of perhaps,
To me shows insecure.

The wealth I had contented me;
If 't was a meaner size,
Then I had counted it until
It pleased my narrow eyes

Better than larger values,
However true their show;
This timid life of evidence
Keeps pleading, "I don't know."

There came a day at summer's full
Entirely for me;
I thought that such were for the saints,
Where revelations be.

The sun, as common, went abroad,
The flowers, accustomed, blew,
As if no soul the solstice passed
That maketh all things new.

The time was scarce profaned by speech;
The symbol of a word
Was needless, as a sacrament
The wardrobe of our Lord.

Each was to each the sealed church,
Permitted to commune this time,
Lest we too awkward show
At supper of the Lamb.

The hours slid fast, as hours will,
Clutched tight by greedy hands;
So faces on two decks look back,
Bound to opposing lands.

And so, when all the time had failed,
Without external sound,
Each bound the other's crucifix,
We gave no other bond.

Sufficient troth that we shall rise—
Deposed, at length, the grave—
To that new marriage, justified
Through Calvaries of Love!

There is a word
Which bears a sword
  Can pierce an armèd man.
It hurls its barbed syllables,—
  At once is mute again.
But where it fell
The saved will tell
  On patriotic day,
Some epauletted brother
  Gave his breath away.

Wherever runs the breathless sun,
  Wherever roams the day,
There is its noiseless onset,
  There is its victory!

Behold the keenest marksman!
  The most accomplished shot!
Time's sublimest target
  Is a soul 'forgot'!

There's a certain slant of light,
On winter afternoons,
That oppresses, like the weight
Of cathedral tunes.

Heavenly hurt it gives us;
We can find no scar,
But internal difference
Where the meanings are.

None may teach it anything,
'T is the seal, despair,—
An imperial affliction
Sent us of the air.

When it comes, the landscape listens,
Shadows hold their breath;
When it goes, 't is like the distance
On the look of death.

There's been a death in the opposite house
  As lately as to-day.
I know it by the numb look
  Such houses have alway.

The neighbors rustle in and out,
  The doctor drives away.
A window opens like a pod,
  Abrupt, mechanically;

Somebody flings a mattress out,—
  The children hurry by;
They wonder if It died on that,—
  I used to when a boy.

The minister goes stiffly in
  As if the house were his,
And he owned all the mourners now,
  And little boys besides;

And then the milliner, and the man
  Of the appalling trade,
To take the measure of the house.
  There'll be that dark parade

Of tassels and of coaches soon;
  It's easy as a sign,—
The intuition of the news
  In just a country town.

These are the days when birds come back,
A very few, a bird or two,
To take a backward look.

These are the days when skies put on
The old, old sophistries of June,—
A blue and gold mistake.

Oh, fraud that cannot cheat the bee,
Almost thy plausibility
Induces my belief,

Till ranks of seeds their witness bear,
And softly through the altered air
Hurries a timid leaf!

Oh, sacrament of summer days,
Oh, last communion in the haze,
Permit a child to join,

Thy sacred emblems to partake,
Thy consecrated bread to break,
Taste thine immortal wine!

This world is not conclusion;
  A sequel stands beyond,
Invisible, as music,
  But positive, as sound.
It beckons and it baffles;
  Philosophies don't know,
And through a riddle, at the last,
  Sagacity must go.
To guess it puzzles scholars;
  To gain it, men have shown
Contempt of generations,
  And crucifixion known.

' T is little I could care for pearls
  Who own the ample sea;
Or brooches, when the Emperor
  With rubies pelteth me;

Or gold, who am the Prince of Mines;
  Or diamonds, when I see
A diadem to fit a dome
  Continual crowning me.

'T is sunrise, little maid, hast thou
  No station in the day?
'T was not thy wont to hinder so,—
  Retrieve thine industry.

'T is noon, my little maid, alas!
  And art thou sleeping yet?
The lily waiting to be wed,
  The bee, dost thou forget?

My little maid, 't is night; alas,
  That night should be to thee
Instead of morning! Hadst thou broached
  Thy little plan to me,
Dissuade thee if I could not, sweet,
  I might have aided thee.

To disappear enhances—
The Man that runs away
Is tinctured for an instant
With Immortality

But yesterday a Vagrant—
Today in Memory lain
With superstitious value
We tamper with "Again"

But "Never" far as Honor
Withdraws the Worthless thing
And impotent to cherish
We hasten to adorn—

Of Death the sternest function
That just as we discern
The Excellence defies us—
Securest gathered then

The Fruit perverse to plucking,
But leaning to the Sight
With the extatic limit
Of unobtained Delight—

To hear an Oriole sing
May be a common thing—
Or only a divine.

It is not of the Bird
Who sings the same, unheard,
As unto Crowd—

The Fashion of the Ear
Attireth that it hear
In Dun, or fair—

So whether it be Rune,
Or whether it be none
Is of within.

The "Tune is in the Tree—"
The Skeptic—showeth me—
"No Sir! In Thee!"

To learn the Transport by the Pain—
As Blind Men learn the sun!
To die of thirst—suspecting
That Brooks in Meadows run!

To stay the homesick—homesick feet
Upon a foreign shore—
Haunted by native lands, the while—
And blue—beloved air!

This is the Sovreign Anguish!
This—the signal wo!
These are the patient "Laureates"
Whose voices—trained—below—

Ascend in ceaseless Carol—
Inaudible, indeed,
To us—the duller scholars
Of the Mysterious Bard!

To lose thee—sweeter than to gain
All other hearts I knew.
'Tis true the drought is destitute,
But then, I had the dew!

The Caspian has its realms of sand,
Its other realm of sea.
Without the sterile perquisite,
No Caspian could be.

You cannot put a fire out;
  A thing that can ignite
Can go, itself, without a fan
  Upon the slowest night.

You cannot fold a flood
  And put it in a drawer,—
Because the winds would find it out,
  And tell your cedar floor.

Afterword

In April 1862 Emily Dickinson wrote a letter to journalist Thomas Wentworth Higginson and sent him a few of her poems. He responded cordially, and their continuing exchange of letters (only her half is intact) seems to have been eminently polite. When Higginson asked her to send him a photograph of herself, she replied, "Could you believe me—without? I had no portrait, now, but am small, like the Wren, and my Hair is bold, like the Chestnut Bur—and my eyes, like the Sherry in the Glass, that the Guest leaves—would this do as well?" A close look at this witty refusal is revealing.

With or without a portrait, Dickinson is a bit hard to believe. The only surviving picture of her—a daguerrotype of a seventeen-year old girl looking seriously at the camera and holding a flower—has fixed her in the popular imagination as a delicate, flower-like child. But when Dickinson refused Higginson's request for a picture, she was 31 years old and had already written hundreds of poems. And as her verbal self-portrait to Higginson hints, in her own estimation she was neither delicate nor a child. If Dickinson admits to being "small" in stature, she specifies that she is "small like the Wren," a diminutive songbird with a big voice. If her "Hair is bold" in color, she suggests that this boldness carries over to her temperament, hinting at a stubborn tendency to stick to things like a burr. Her eyes are not merely sherry-colored, but "like the Sherry in the Glass, that the Guest leaves." Why the extra details in this metaphor? Why does the poet use such a roundabout way to inform Higginson that she has auburn hair and hazel eyes? The half-inch of sherry left at the bottom of a glass looks like eyes—a household detail becomes a striking metaphor. "That the Guest leaves": this odd phrase in Dickinson's self-portrait suggests the poet's concern with remnants, remainders, crumbs, her theme of the powerful knowledge that comes with deprivation. Tidying up after her father's guests, Dickinson found herself reflected in the minutest domestic chores. She made poetry from what others discarded as insignificant.

Dickinson ends this self-portrait in words with the plea, "Would this do as well?" Will Higginson accept her verbal sketch instead of a photographic image? By posing this question to him, Dickinson invites the man to whom she would sign herself "Your Scholar" to value the kinds of images her poetry can create. She also implies that the true Emily Dickinson is not the woman in a picture, but the sensibility that emerges from a style of writing. This little word-picture of the poet gently chastises Higginson for his literal-minded interest in what she looks like.

Elsewhere, she explicitly cautioned Higginson not to take her poems as autobiographical: "When I state myself, as the Representative of the Verse—it does not mean—me—but a supposed person." If the "I" that speaks so many of the poems cannot reliably be identified as Dickinson herself, where is she—the biographical Emily Elizabeth Dickinson of Amherst, Massachusetts—in her poems?

She is everywhere, and nowhere. Some of her self-portraits (or portraits of one side of her character, or of what she'd like to be) may be found in descriptions of nature. Her portrait of the hemlock tree which "thrives on cold" suggests the poet's own ability to thrive on little, and implies that her austere, unflowery poems share the "austerity" of the hemlock. "I think the hemlock likes to stand / Upon a marge of snow," the poem begins, and Dickinson likes to understand these natural creatures that crave cold, these unrecognized heroes of renunciation. A spider's self-reliant weaving is another model for Dickinson's own poetry stitchery ("A spider sewed at night").

By musing on the self-sustaining power of natural elements, Dickinson may reflect on her own astonishing gifts:

You cannot put a fire out;
  A thing that can ignite
Can go, itself, without a fan
  Upon the darkest night.

You cannot fold a flood
  And put it in a drawer,—
Because the winds would find it out,
  And tell your cedar floor.

What clues enable us to find a self-portrait in this poem? Some clues come from other poems: one compares a soul to a white-hot furnace ("Dare you see a soul at the white heat?"). And like "The reticent volcano keeps" (discussed below), this poem begins with fire and ends with telling a secret. While fire and water might be seen as opposites (since water can douse fire), this poem pairs them together as unstoppable, unconcealable forces.

The mention of finding out and telling in the second stanza is curious. What is kept in a drawer and eventually is found out? It is hard not to think of the hundreds of sheets of folded letter paper filled with poems that Dickinson kept in her drawer. Did she believe that eventually her poems would be published, as surely as a flood would leak from a drawer? Or is the flood an image for the flow of creativity as the poet experiences it? Acknowledging that speculations about an afterlife prompted many poems, Dickinson once called immortality her "Flood subject." We may find the metaphor suits our experience as readers as well. Like fire and flood, Dickinson's poems cannot be contained—the more you think about them, the more they spread and unfold, the more questions they ignite.

Such startling images of flood, fire, explosion, and volcanic destruction may indicate how her dazzling creative power felt to Dickinson herself. She once defined poetry in terms of its violent bodily effects on the reader: "If I read a book [and] it makes my whole body so cold no fire can ever warm me I know *that* is poetry. If I feel physically as if the top of my head were taken off, I know *that* is poetry. These are the only way I know it. Is there any other way [?]"

Her portraits of admirable independence are not all violent, though. One poem twists the old saying "A rolling stone gathers no moss"—a proverb generally used to recommend change and variety in life. It is hard to imagine an outwardly more changeless life than Dickinson's, but she seems to share the pleasure she imagines is enjoyed by the proverbial rolling stone:

> How happy is the little stone
> That rambles in the road alone,
> And doesn't care about careers.

Dickinson made a career of not having one. Since her poetic rambling was private, she never got in the rut of the conservative business of the literary professional. With an ideal self-sufficiency, the stone

> Independent as the sun,
> Associates or glows alone,
> Fulfilling absolute decree
> In casual simplicity.

This seems an odd claim—that a (hard, little) stone is like the (huge, blazing) sun. But Dickinson admires anything that fulfills its own nature without being coerced or artificial. The stone's "coat of elemental brown" is not a coat of paint, but simply the natural color "A passing universe put on": the smallest stone has a relation to the whole universe. Did Dickinson believe she too was fulfilling some "absolute decree?" Probably not—her work is too riddled with doubt to put much faith in absolutes. But she too felt that she was touched by the passing universe and received "bulletins from immortality." She was small—but like the tuneful wren; she was small—but like a stone whose independence puts it on a par with the sun.

It's necessary to be cautious and tactful, of course, in interpreting Dickinson's poems about trees and stones as poems about the poet herself. But the same discretion is called for in reading poems that seem to be transparently about the private emotions of the poem's speaker. Much ink has been spilled on the question of a supposed disappointment in love that called forth some of the more anguished lyrics. Even if the hard knot of these tantalizing poems were to be undone with one tug of the right secret thread, a basic mystery would remain. For not every thwarted life yields a treasure of remarkable poetry. Whatever emotional attachments Dickinson did or did not form, one thing is clear: Her chief love was the language of poetry, and that was a fruitful, sustained pairing for both parties.

Dickinson's life was unexciting compared to the wide-ranging, roistering careers of such nineteenth-century American writers as Poe, Melville, Stephen Crane, Mark Twain, and Whitman. Perhaps Dickinson looks less peculiar if she is considered part of another strain of New England writing. Her life seems more like the home-keeping quiet of Nathaniel Hawthorne, or the deliberately narrowed life of Henry David Thoreau at Walden Pond. But Dickinson's outwardly uneventful life was typical for women in her day, while these literary New Englanders made a choice to forgo some of the opportunities beyond the household that were available to men.

As many of Dickinson's poems argue, the best way truly to appreciate anything is to be denied it. Some literary sensibilities find their material at sea, some at home. There is no single path an American writer's life must follow.

It may be time to stop asking the question that has haunted Dickinson's readers: How can remarkable poems emerge from such an ordinary life? It's not really a mystery: many poems reflect on ordinary life in such a way that it seems extraordinary. Daily events like the sunset, a storm, a change in the air that hints of the arrival of spring: all of these can be the occasion for surprising reflections.

How did Dickinson's poems result from her life? The question itself is based on a false assumption, that only a varied public life can prompt writing that reflects a wealth of beliefs and feelings. Dickinson knew that every human heart was a fiery forge. Like Thoreau, who boasted that he had travelled widely in Concord, Dickinson ranged far afield while remaining in Amherst. The question also presupposes that poems register or reflect the happenings of a writer's life. A reasonable assumption, surely—but Dickinson has a way of turning our common sense intuitions inside out. In Dickinson's life, the act of writing was itself the crucial event. Three decades spent writing almost 1800 poems hardly add up to an ordinary life, even if spent in one room in one small town.

And for Dickinson words themselves were remarkable things. The poems describe books as miraculously liberating, and reading as sacramental: "He ate and drank the precious Words." Getting mail requires a private ritual, so intense is the sensation of receiving another's voice on paper ("The way I read a letter's this"). Why go whaling, river-boating, or to war when the simple act of reading a letter can yield such heightened sensations?

Reading Dickinson's poetry may provide a spectrum of

sensations (shock, frustration, pleasure, puzzlement, recognition, wonder). And reading even a small selection of Dickinson's poems involves playing favorites. There are certain to be some poems in this book that you like more than others, and that's as it should be. To be a reader of Dickinson is to accumulate your own personal anthology of Dickinson poems.

Poems that seemed opaque the first few times you read them may grow less shadowy in the light shed on them by other poems. Clustering poems together is a useful method for reading any poet; for Dickinson it can be essential in order to understand the most impenetrable and mysterious of them. A look at one poem through the lenses of others may suggest further directions for reading.

> The reticent volcano keeps
> His never slumbering plan;
> Confided are his projects pink
> To no precarious man.
>
> If nature will not tell the tale
> Jehovah told to her
> Can human nature not survive
> Without a listener?
>
> Admonished by her buckled lips
> Let every babbler be
> The only secret people keep
> Is Immortality.

What is this poem about? Editors of the first posthumous collections of Dickinson's poems grouped them in loose categories (Nature, Love, Time and Eternity). The poem begins by pointing out a feature of the natural world, and in that sense might seem to belong with poems about flowers, birds, and sunsets. But Dickinson never saw a volcano; that was not included in even her scrupulous inventory of the grounds of her Amherst house.

And this volcano is described as though it contained not a dangerous mass of molten rock, but a secret. Volcanos are dangerous because they may erupt without warning; here a volcano's eruption is implicitly compared to speech. When the volcano talks, people really listen; his revelations are sudden and devastating. A volcano "confides" his fiery "pink" "project" rarely, but powerfully. The second stanza lists another paragon of a tight-lipped temperament: nature herself doesn't tell us what "Jehovah" told her. Nature is secretive, no blabbermouth of God's confidences.

The third stanza points to a lesson for people taught by these exemplars of natural reticence. The last lines imply that people talk too much, but despite their constantly blathering to satisfy their unrelenting need to find listeners, they never tell us what happens to them beyond the grave. Just when those lifelong chatterboxes and tattletales get to where they really could tell us something we want to know, they fall silent: "The only secret people keep / Is Immortality."

The tone of this warning to "babblers" shares the wry earnestness of her remark to Higginson that she avoided people because "they speak of sacred things, and frighten my dog." To better understand the poem that begins "The reticent volcano," it will help to read it beside other short poems concerned with words and speech. One poem compares a word to a weapon: "There is a word / Which bears a sword." How can we find the dangerous blade hidden in a word? Look at *sword*: it contains the word *word*. A coincidence? Idle wordplay? (Watch her perform the same trick in "We wish the *ear* had not a *heart* / So dangerously near" ["The saddest noise, the sweetest noise"; my italics].) Dickinson seems to have stared at words long and hard until they yielded such secrets. She spoke of certain words that "glow" like "sapphires," words that, she said, make her "lift my hat" when she saw them on the page. Did her awareness of words' jewel-like glow and their "barbed syllables" keep her poems short? If words have such power, a poet must indeed be like a "reticent volcano," keeping explosive resources bottled up, and dispensing them in prudent doses.

One of Dickinson's best known poems about words is also one of her briefest: "A word is dead / When it is said / Some say. / I say it just / Begins to live / That day." Here again we see Dickinson putting a spin on a popular saying. The idea that a word once spoken can never be taken back is a proverbial caution against speaking rashly. The spoken word is born, not killed. Recall her request to Higginson to judge if her poems were "alive." A successful poem, in Dickinson's view, was like a living, breathing thing. That you are reading her poems now suggests she was right.

—Debra Fried,
Cornell University

Index of First Lines